# Raise the Bar

## Grades 6-8

## Guitar

Teaching Notes written
by Anders Rye

Published by
Trinity College London Press
trinitycollege.com

Registered in England
Company no. 09726123

Printed in England by Caligraving Ltd.

# Contents

# Teaching Notes – Grade 6

## Study in A Major (Carcassi)

*Study in A Major* is from a well-known collection of 25 progressive studies for guitar that Carcassi published around 1852. Each of these studies focuses on a specific technical area of development and they gradually increase in difficulty.

This study (no. 23 in the series) is a busy and fast moving piece in $\frac{12}{8}$. The focus is on slurs and position changes so make these as fluent and smooth as possible. The quaver rhythm is continuous throughout so there is no time to rest for the picking hand, particularly at tempo **allegro**, but keep the quavers even with a triplet feel. This piece has to be played with pace and forward movement and you may want to use a metronome to practise with. Start slowly and work on increasing the tempo in smaller sections at a time without losing the fluency.

## Étude (Coste)

Napoléon Coste was a French guitar virtuoso initially taught by his mother but was later a student of Fernando Sor. Coste spent much of his time in Paris where he befriended other well-known guitarists and composers such as Carcassi, Aguado and Carulli but an accident in 1863 left him with a broken arm and ended his performing career. This étude no. 4 is from *25 Études de genre* – one of Coste's most important works. He often composed for 7-string guitar and these pieces were originally intended for such an instrument.

This beautiful piece is graceful and almost choral-like. The picking hand has to be quite delicate as you will need to bring out the different voices so this is a good exercise in controlling the weight of each finger. Try to let the chords and notes really sing out and use the dynamic markings for colour and effect.

## El Velorio (Cervantes)

*El Velorio* means 'the wake' and it is one of 38 *Danzas Cubanas* (Cuban dances) by the Cuban composer Ignacio Cervantes who was just nine years old when he composed the first one. All the *danzas* were composed for piano and cover a range of moods and emotions from playful and humorous to poignant and melancholic. Most *danzas* are 32 bars long, made up of two 16-bar sections, in $\frac{2}{4}$ time signature and with a key change in the second half.

*El Velorio* has been arranged for guitar in the book *6 Danzas Cubanas* and it follows the above structure with a key change from A minor to F major, along with another typical *danza* characteristic which is the use of rising and falling thirds. Apart from the key change, the rhythm also becomes more varied and complex in the second half so there is variation in rhythm as well as in harmony.

## Andantino Campestre (Castelnuovo-Tedesco)

*Andantino Campestre* was sadly one of the last compositions by the Italian composer Mario Castelnuovo-Tedesco. It was to be part of a four-book series of progressive study pieces named *Appunti* (meaning sketches or notes) but, due to Castelnuovo-Tedesco's untimely death, only two books were published and the complete work was never finished. Castelnuovo-Tedesco, who scored some 200 Hollywood films in his career, was also a prolific composer for guitar. *Appunti* was undertaken on the suggestion of guitarist Ruggero Chiesa.

*Andantino Campestre* is known as 'The Song of the Reapers' (*campestre* meaning rural) and it is taken from the first book of *Appunti* entitled 'Intervals'. This gentle piece focuses specifically on thirds with a melody in two voices. *Espr. cantando* means 'expressive singing' and notice how the crescendos and diminuendos follow the rise and fall in pitch and make the phrases ebb and flow. The thirds are sometimes played along the same strings to give a soft and round tone but aim for an even and balanced sound whether you move along or across strings.

## Spanish Guitar Blues (Byrd)

Charlie Byrd was an American jazz guitarist who studied classical guitar under Andrés Segovia but he was probably best known for the album *Jazz Samba* which he recorded with saxophonist Stan Getz. Their success in fusing jazz with Brazilian samba helped popularise a genre of music that became known as *bossa nova* (new wave) and the album reached number one on the American Billboard pop charts in 1963.

*Spanish Guitar Blues* is a light-hearted twist on a standard blues but it still follows a 12-bar pattern and has a shuffle/swing feel. The 12-bar structure is repeated throughout the piece with a number of variations so that the chords sometimes are arpeggiated and sometimes played together with a walking bass line. Keep the swing feel relaxed and fluent without sounding rigid. The repeats allow plenty of opportunity to experiment with variation in tone and dynamics.

## Hommage à Ravel (Wills)

Arthur Wills is an English organist, composer and former professor at the Royal Academy of Music, London. He was Director of Music at Ely Cathedral for many years and has composed numerous orchestral and instrumental works as well as many choral compositions and an opera. *Hommage à Ravel* is from the book *Easy Modern Guitar Music* and it is tribute to the French composer Maurice Ravel who is most famous for his *Boléro*.

The harmonies are quite complex in this piece and can sound strange and unfamiliar at first. This is a modern composition so you may also find that chords and patterns are unusual and less predictable than with traditional classical composers like Sor or Giuliani. The tempo is slow and expressive and there are many changes in dynamics, as well as harmony, to create colours and contrast. Practise slowly at first and give your ears and fingers time to get used to the sound and movements.

# Study in A Major

## op. 60 no. 23

Edited by Michael Lewin

Matteo Carcassi
(1792–1853)

D.C. al Fine

# Étude

## op. 38 no. 4

Napoleon Coste
(1806-1883)

# El Velorio

## from *6 Danzas Cubanas*

Arr. By Jesús Ortega

Ignacio Cervantes
(1847-1905)

# Andantino Campestre

## Appunti no. 4

Mario Castelnuovo-Tedesco
(1895-1968)

# Spanish Guitar Blues

Charlie Byrd
(1925-1999)

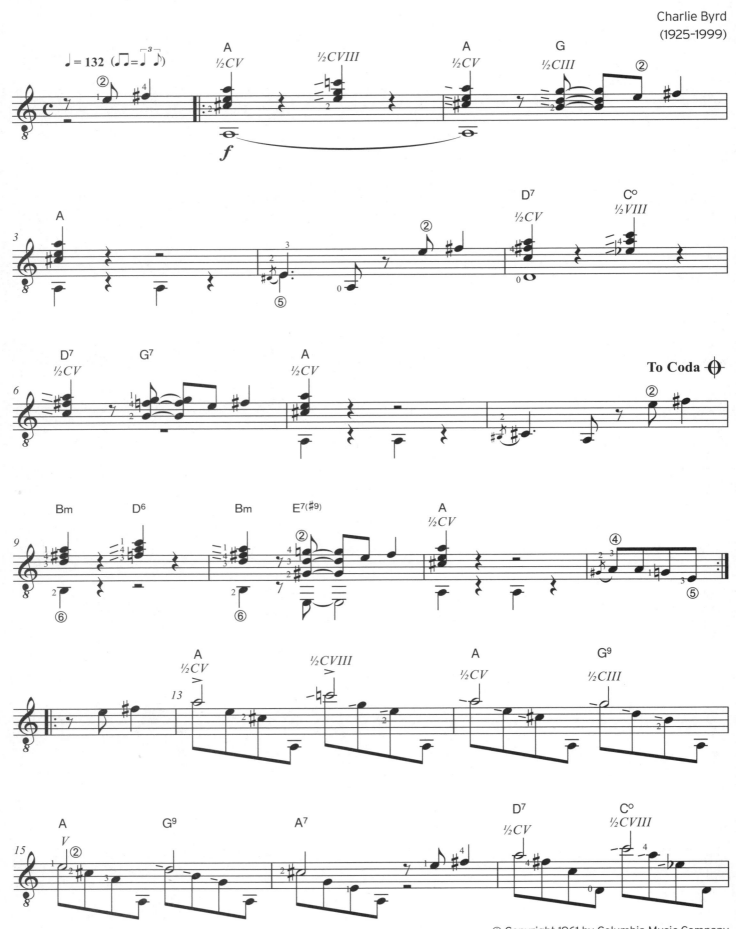

# Hommage à Ravel

Arthur Wills
(b. 1926)

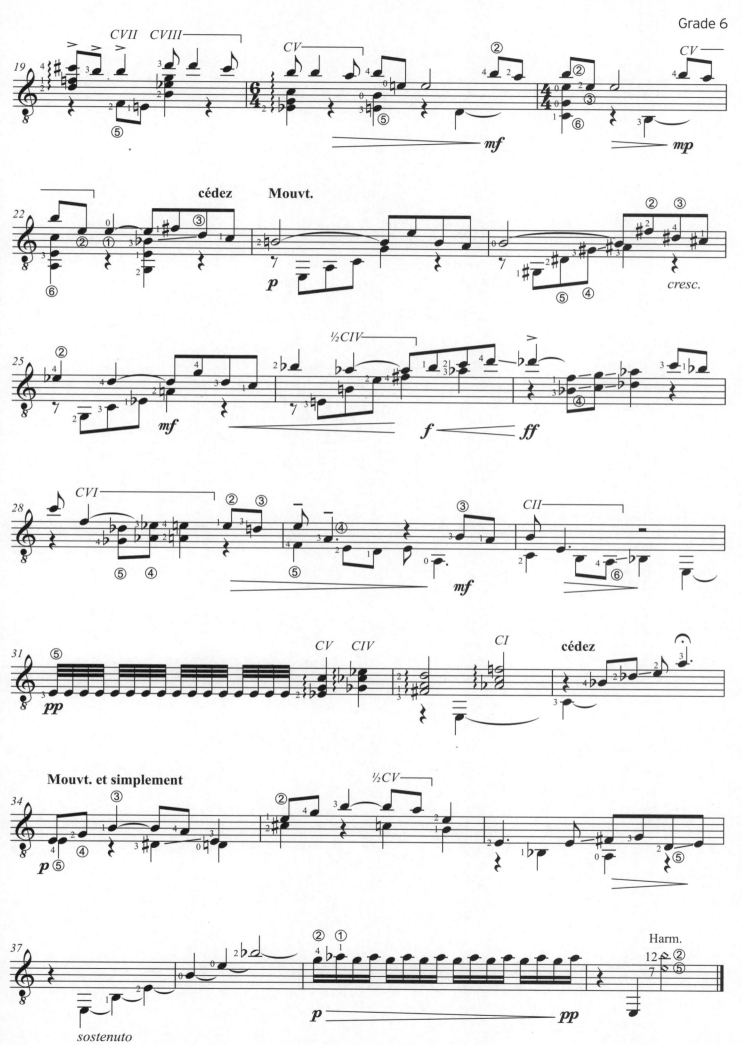

(Blank page to facilitate page turns)

# Teaching Notes – Grade 7

## Fantasia (Holborne)

Very little is known about the life of Antony Holborne, though it is assumed that he served under Queen Elizabeth I in some capacity. It is certain, however, that Holborne was held in high regard by his contemporary John Dowland, and his most significant contribution to musical literature was the publication of 65 pieces in *Pavans, Galliards, Almains and other short Aeirs, both grave and light, in five parts, for Viols, Violins, or other Musicall Winde Instruments* in 1599.

This *Fantasia* was originally written for the bandora, a stringed instrument similar to a bass cittern: a *fantasia* (fantasy) is a musical idea that is free in form and often based on improvisation, hence the name. The way the voices interweave, overlap and imitate each other is typical for music from this period and this piece is a good exercise in phrasing. Try to keep a balance between the voices and bring out each phrase separately and clearly.

## Sonata (Scarlatti)

Domenico Scarlatti was born in Naples in 1685, the same year as Bach and Handel, but is perhaps not nearly as celebrated as his Baroque contemporaries and may be slightly overlooked as a composer. He did, however, compose 555 keyboard sonatas, most of them while working at the Royal courts in Spain and Portugal. Scarlatti's sonatas were heavily influenced by Spanish music and culture and his music is often described as imitating folk (flamenco) guitar techniques and expressing the essence of Spain better than any native composer. The present *Sonata K208* was written for harpsichord but has been arranged for guitar, and is one of Scarlatti's best known sonatas in the *cantabile* (singable) style.

This is a beautiful and elegant piece in two parts, and only 25 bars long. The texture is simple with a lyrical melody line and the accompanying bass playing crotchets throughout. Scarlatti explores the use of suspensions and creates tension by using both syncopated rhythms and chromatic notes. Make sure that the slurs are clear and take particular care when executing the trills, turns and mordents, all of which are typical of the Baroque era.

## Mazurka in G (Tárrega)

A *mazurka* is a Polish folk dance in $\frac{3}{4}$ time, the name originating from the Mazovia region in Poland. Several classical composers have written mazurkas, but the best known are probably by Fréderic Chopin who wrote more than 50 for solo piano. The dance became popular outside Poland in the 19th century and there are many variations on a *mazurka* in different parts of the world. Traditionally, stylistic characteristics include a dotted quaver and semiquaver on the first beat and crotchets on beats two and three.

Tárrega's lovely *Mazurka in G* (or *Mazurka en Sol*) opens exactly in the way described above but is slower and more *cantabile* than a traditional version. The structure follows an AABBA form with each section being 16 bars long and the B section is slightly slower (**poco meno**) and sweet (*dolce*). You can play closer to the fretboard (sul tasto) to create a rounder and 'sweeter' sound. There is also much use of **ritardando** throughout the whole piece so let that help shape the phrasing and make it expressive and reflective.

## Barcarola (Julia Florida) (Barrios Mangoré)

Agustín Barrios Mangoré was a virtuoso guitarist and composer born in Paraguay in 1885. He is now considered one of the greatest performers and guitar composers of all time but his music was virtually forgotten for decades after his death in 1944. Barrios Mangoré was one of the first guitarists to make gramophone recordings and his concerts were legendary. For a while he assumed a new stage identity and performed in traditional Paraguayan costume under the name of Nitsuga (*Agustín* backwards) Mangoré.

A *barcarola* is a folk song sung by Venetian gondoliers (barca means boat in Italian) in $\frac{6}{8}$ time. The meter indicates the rhythm of the gondolier's stroke and first two bars of this piece perfectly evoke the rolling movement of waves. The subtitle is *Julia Florida* and is dedicated to one of Barrios Mangoré's pupils, Julia Martinez de Rodriguez, whom he was very fond of and may have had a love affair with. What is certain though, is that this beautiful and elegant piece is intensely romantic, and the melody and harmonies are laden with emotion, so try your best to bring these out.

## Berceuse (Brouwer)

A *berceuse* is a lullaby and this piece is also known as *Cancion de Cuna* or *Drume Negrita* and is from Brouwer's *Dos Temas Populares Cubanos* published in 1968. Brouwer is a very productive Cuban composer who plays several instruments and is also highly regarded world wide as a teacher and conductor.

*Berceuse* is a lovely piece with a simple recurring melody. There are really just two melodic ideas although there is some variation in the middle section. The beginning is played *pizzicato* which is achieved by slightly muting the strings near the bridge with your picking hand. The bass figure in the first bar is echoed up an octave and features throughout the piece between each melodic section and also in the underlying accompaniment. Keep the melody legato and balanced with the accompanying bass and use the dynamics to create some colour and contrast.

## Smoke Rising (Ryan)

This is a fun and interesting piece to play and explores a range of sounds that you can make on a guitar as well as some unusual techniques. It is taken from a suite of six pieces with the title *Scenes From The Wild West* which can be found on Gary Ryan's album *Worlds Apart*.

**Mean, moody and mysterious** indicates how this piece should be played right from the beginning and you have to imagine an Apache Indian tribe around their campfire. The opening rhythm and percussive *tambor* (tambor means drum) technique perfectly evoke the sound of war drums and tribal dance around the fire. The tricky oblique slurs and harmonics are reminiscent of ephemeral smoke slowly rising and disappearing in the wind. There is a broad dynamic range and the piece comes to a dramatic climax in bar 39 before settling down again towards the end. *Smoke Rising* uses various elements and techniques from flamenco, folk and rock/blues so have fun trying to create all these sounds and effects.

# Fantasia

Antony Holborne
(d. 1602)

# Sonata

## K. 208

Domenico Scarlatti
(1685-1757)

# Mazurka in G

Francisco Tárrega
(1852-1909)

# Barcarola

## Julia Florida

Agustín Barrios Mangoré
(1885-1944)

(Blank page to facilitate page turns)

# Berceuse

from *Dos temas populares cubanos*

Leo Brouwer
(b. 1939)

# Smoke Rising

Gary Ryan
(b. 1969)

(1) Rub the strings over the sound hole using the flesh of the *m* finger.
(2) Fingered notes of the first chord in the bar should be played with an oblique slur (hammered).

(Blank page to facilitate page turns)

# Teaching Notes – Grade 8

## Variations on Les Folies d'Espagne (Sor)

*Les Folies d'Espagne* (Follies of Spain) refers to la Folia which is a compositional framework based on one of the oldest known musical themes. It has been used by many composers over the past centuries and is distinguished as an *early folia* and a *late folia*. Sor based his theme on the *late folia* which follows a specific chord progression, however there are four variations and a minuet included in the original edition. A theme with variations is a great opportunity for composers to showcase their skills and creativity, and it is a fun and educative way for a student to explore a musical idea.

The theme is in E minor and all the variations have thirds as a common feature. The first variation uses thirds moving chromatically in the melody, whereas the other two variations employ thirds in the accompaniment. Each variation differs in nature but try to create some contrast between them by adding dynamics and experiment with varied tone colours.

## El Catalán (Brocá)

José Brocá was a Spanish guitarist and composer from the Romantic period who was born and lived in Catalonia his whole life, and the title of this piece reflects his affiliation with that region. Brocá was allegedly taught by Dionisio Aguado and later went on to teach José Ferrer who dedicated two pieces to him. Brocá wrote around 20 works for guitar and his style is elegant and similar to Tárrega's though written much earlier.

*El Catalán* is a lively waltz which begins in E minor and modulates to G major before ending in E major in the final section. Brocá uses some chromatic suspension in the melody which has to be balanced against the accompaniment, particularly when there is a melody note with a chord. There is a lot of dynamic variation and detail in this piece so be sure to observe those throughout and notice the *caesura* (a brief pause) in bars 50, 66 and 98 which gives a slight pause between phrases.

## Gran Vals (Tárrega)

Tárrega's *Gran Vals* (Great Waltz) is known by millions of people for being the official Nokia ringtone since the 1990s. Specifically, it is the ending of the first 16-bar section but the Nokia version ends on A whereas the original ends on E.

*Gran Vals* is in the key of A major and has four sections in different keys. It modulates to E major and B major returning to E major and finally repeating the first section in A major. The rhythm is a simple and straightforward $\frac{3}{4}$ waltz feel with a strong emphasis on the first beats and crotchets on beat two and three for most parts. The opening *glissando* and the slurs on the higher notes are typical of Tárrega's style, and there are elements, like the prominent bass feature in the B major section, which are reminiscent of some of his other compositions, for example *Rosita*. The piece needs some pace to avoid sounding heavy so be careful not to play it too slowly and keep the melody light and elegant.

## Reboliço (Pernambuco)

João Pernambuco was one of the founders of the Brazilian *choro* style. His real name was João Teixeira Guimarães, and got his name from the Pernambuco region in Brazil where he was born. He came from a humble background and a large family – he had 19 siblings. Pernambuco learned the guitar from watching and listening to street musicians and although he had a success as a musician he never forgot his simple working class roots and worked as a blacksmith in between performing, teaching and composing.

*Reboliço* (meaning disorder or uproar) consists of three different sections arranged in a rondo form as AABBACCA. It is to be played **giocoso** which means merry or joyful and all the sections are in major keys, the main being in A major and the others in E major and D major. The rhythm is syncopated and busy and there is a lot of emphasis on the bass so keep a strong sense of pulse and timing throughout to add character to this piece.

## Preludio (Mompou)

Federico Mompou was a Spanish pianist and composer. *Preludio* is the first of six movements from *Suite Compostelana* in tribute to the Spanish city, Santiago de Compostela, and was inspired by Galician folklore. The suite was written in 1962 and dedicated to Andrés Segovia and incorporates traditional Spanish guitar sounds and modes with contemporary harmony.

*Preludio* has an eerie and ethereal modal or ancient sound to it, yet is highly chromatic with modern sounding chords and arpeggios. The structure is broadly an ABA form with a coda, though the key changes from E minor to A minor in the last section. The piece opens with an inverted pedal point in the high register so keep the picking even before moving down to the lowest note on the guitar. Parts of the middle section are **espressivo** (expressive) or **molto** (very) **espressivo** in contrast to the fast moving chromatic passage. This is an interesting and colourful piece which will require some effort to master, however the process, hopefully, will also be very rewarding.

## Vals Venezolano No. 2 (Lauro)

*Vals Venezolano No. 2* is from a series of four Venezuelan waltzes and Lauro named this piece *Andreina* after his niece. These pieces are among some of Lauro's most popular compositions and the guitarist John Williams once called him the 'Strauss of the guitar' (Johan Strauss II was known as the 'The Waltz King').

This piece is in two parts and the meter is slightly ambiguous combining $\frac{6}{8}$ and $\frac{3}{4}$ so it is important to get both the timing and feel right. Lauro's works are always technically demanding and it can be challenging to keep the melody clear and legato through some of the position changes, especially with a bit of pace. Make a smooth transition between the harmonics and the open strings and let the bass notes ring for as long as possible. Try to inject some of the Latin spirit into this waltz and keep it uptempo without sounding too heavy.

# Variations (on 'Les Folies d'Espagne') and Minuet

## op. 15a

Edited by Michael Lewin

Fernando Sor
(1778-1839)

# El Catalán

José Brocá
(1805-1882)

**Allegretto** ♪ = 144

# Gran Vals

Francisco Tárrega
(1852–1909)

# Reboliço

João Pernambuco
(1883–1947)

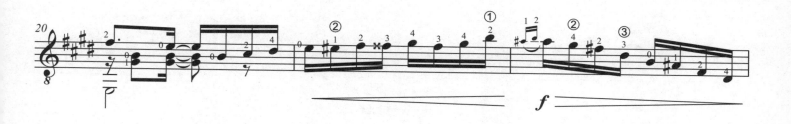

Grade 8

# Preludio
## Suite Compostelana

Federico Mompou
(1893-1987)

A tempo

# Vals Venezolano No. 2

## (Venezuelan Waltz)

Edited by Alirio Diaz

Antonio Lauro
(1917-1986)

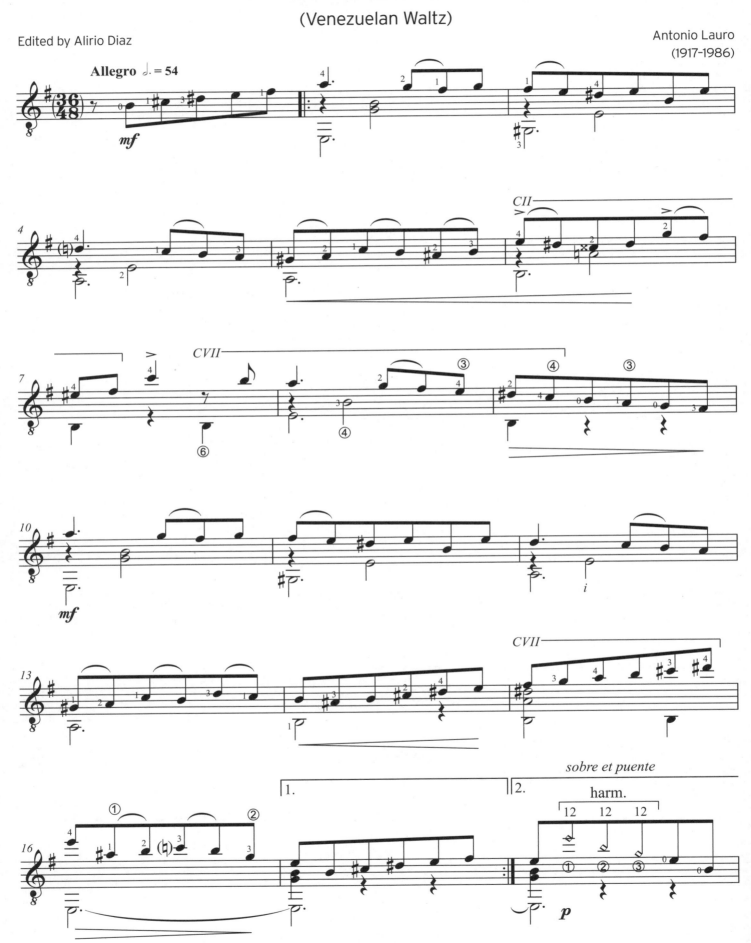

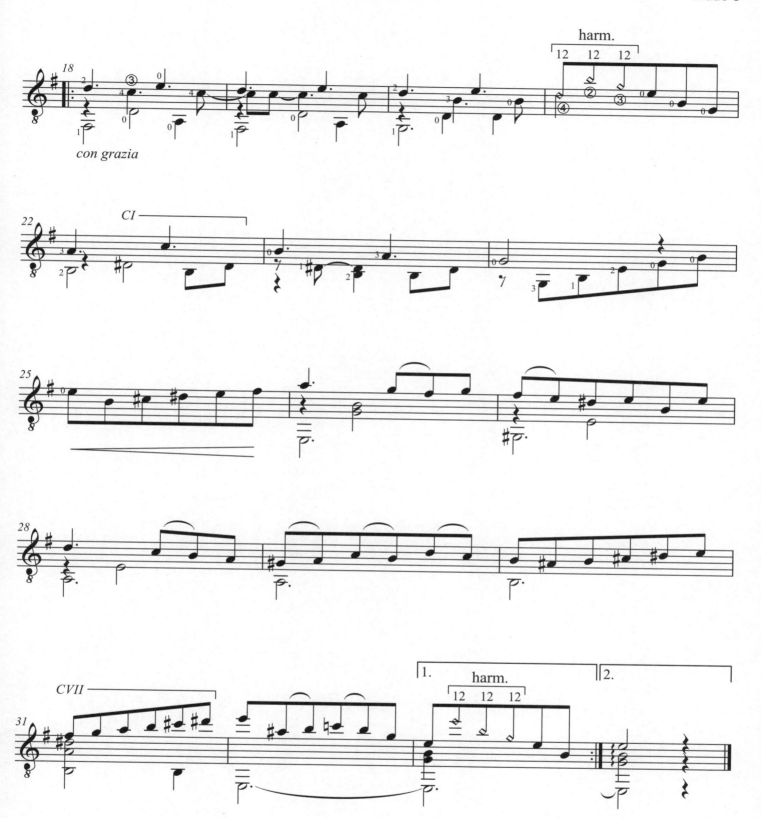